TRUE CAT STORIES
IN BASIC VOCABULARY

By

MARGUERITE P. DOLCH

Illustrated by

MARGUERITE DOLCH

DLM
Teaching
Resources
One DLM Park • Allen, Texas 75002

Library of Congress Cataloging in Publication Data

Dolch, Marguerite Pierce, 1891—
   True cat stories

   (The Basic vocabulary series)
   SUMMARY: Twenty-one true stories illustrating
some of the peculiar characteristics of cats.
   1. Cats—Legends and stories. [1. Cats—Fiction.
2. Short stories] I. Title.
PZ10.3.D71094Tr   [E]   75-2146
ISBN 0-8116-2516-8

Foreword

Most people love cats. This book is full of true stories about cats. That is, the names and some details may have been changed, but the things the cats did are true. We know this because every story is the rewriting of a true story taken from a newspaper or other news report. In fact, there were so many wonderful things that cats have done that we had a great deal of trouble picking out the few that we were able to put into this book.

Anyone who knows and loves cats knows that cats do and think just as they do in these stories. Of course cats do not use words. But they do think of people and places, and they do know what people around them are thinking and feeling.

Many men and women have written books about their cats. If you like these Cat Stories go to the library and get some books about cats.

So to all cat lovers and to all cats we dedicate this book.

MARGUERITE P. DOLCH

iii

Contents

Jasper, Come Back

Mr. Mason and his family were driving from New York to St. Louis. The children, Susan and Joe, were in the back seat with Jasper, a big black and white cat.

One day Mr. Mason was driving on a winding road. Suddenly around a curve came a big truck almost on the wrong side of the road.

Mr. Mason turned the car into the bank at the side of the road.

Everything happened very quickly. Jasper, the big black and white cat, jumped out of the car window. He ran away among the trees as fast as he could go.

Susan and Joe got out of the car and ran after Jasper calling, "Jasper, Jasper, come back!" But Jasper was so frightened that he ran on and on.

Mr. and Mrs. Mason got out of the car and went into the woods calling, "Jasper, come back!"

But they could not find Jasper.

The family got back into the car. The children were crying for they loved Jasper very much.

"We will have to go on to St. Louis," said Mr. Mason. "I have a job there to do and I must be there tomorrow."

"Do not cry," said Mrs. Mason. "In a few weeks we will be driving back to New York along this same road. We will stop and hunt for Jasper again."

Mrs. Mason whispered to Mr. Mason, "I don't think we will ever see Jasper again."

When the family got to St. Louis, Mr. Mason was very busy with his new job. Mrs. Mason and the children had a good time in the city.

Susan and Joe went to the zoo in Forest Park. When they saw the black panther, they thought of Jasper and were very sad.

When Mr. Mason finished his job in St. Louis, the family got into the car and started the long drive back to New York. As they were driving along, Joe called out, "This is where we lost Jasper."

Suddenly Mr. Mason stopped the car. There on the bank beside the road sat a black and white cat. It was a very thin and hungry looking cat. But it was Jasper.

Mr. Mason opened the car door, and the children rushed out. But Jasper ran and jumped into the car. He had found his family.

There are many stories about cats who find their way home after being lost. Jasper was a cat who did not try to go home. He waited for his family to find him.

Tom, the Actor

Tom lived in a theater. He was loved by all the workmen and all the actors. The actors thought that Tom brought them good luck.

One night Tom walked into a play. Just before the curtain came down, Tom walked across the stage and seated himself before the stage fireplace.

The actor and actress who were on the stage were very much surprised. But they went on with the play.

Tom just sat before the fireplace. He washed first one paw and then the other paw.

When the curtain went down, the people in the audience clapped and clapped.

The actor and the actress came before the curtain and bowed. But the audience still clapped and clapped.

The director of the play put Tom into the actress's arms and she took him before the curtain. And how the audience clapped for the new actor.

That is how Tom became an actor.

The director of the play knew that somehow he must get Tom to act in the play. A cat sitting before the fireplace was just what the play needed.

The next day nobody could get Tom to sit before the stage fireplace and wash his paws. The director did not know what to do.

Then the boy who looked after Tom and fed him said, "Tom is a good cat, but he doesn't know how to be an actor. He just knows how to catch mice. If I had a mouse, I could get Tom to sit in front of the fireplace."

"We will get a mouse for Tom every night," said the director. "See if you can get Tom to sit before the fireplace."

The boy made a little hole in the stage fireplace. Every night he hid behind the fireplace with a mouse tied to a string. And Tom sat before the fireplace watching that mouse. Tom thought he would surely catch that mouse.

One night the mouse got away. It ran across the stage. The actress was afraid of mice. She forgot all about the play and jumped upon a chair.

The curtain had to come down. The audience was laughing and laughing.

Every night Tom watched that mouse but he never caught it.

Tom was glad when the play ended. Now he just sleeps in his box in the back of the theater. At night when no one is in the theater, Tom catches mice.

The Green Parrot

This is a story about a French cat. She belonged to a writer. The cat sat on the man's lap while he wrote his stories. She followed him like a dog when he walked in the garden.

The cat even sat upon a chair by the table. The man and the cat ate their meals together.

The cat's name was Madam Theophile. But we will call her "Madam" for short.

One day a friend of the writer came to see him.

"I am going on a trip and I don't know what to do with my parrot while I am away," said the friend.

"I will keep your parrot while you are away," said the writer.

"That is very good of you," said the friend. "But Polly talks a lot. She may keep you from writing your stories."

"I am sure that a parrot will not keep me from writing," said the writer.

And so a green parrot came to live in the house with Madam.

Madam was surprised to see this strange looking bird.

All day long Madam sat and watched the parrot in its cage.

She must have thought that this strange looking bird was some sort of a green chicken. Madam knew that chickens were good to eat. But how could she get this green chicken out of its cage.

Polly was very much afraid. Her feathers all stood out. She knew that the cat was thinking that a bird was good to eat.

Polly climbed high upon her perch and looked down at Madam.

Madam walked around and around the stand that held the cage. Madam's tail went from side to side. She half closed her eyes. She was very angry.

Then just as Madam was about to give a big jump, the parrot cried in a loud voice, "Have you had your breakfast? Have you had your breakfast?"

Madam was never so surprised in all of her life. She stopped and looked at the parrot. This green chicken talked like a man.

Then the parrot said in a loud voice, "What did you have for breakfast?"

"This was not a bird," thought Madam. "This green chicken was a strange man."

Madam looked at her master. He was laughing. Madam did not want to be laughed at. She ran away as fast as she could. She ran under the bed and stayed there all day.

From that day, Madam would have nothing to do with the green chicken that talked like a man.

Mary

Mr. Jack had a restaurant. He was a kindly man and everybody that worked in the restaurant liked Mr. Jack.

One day Mr. Jack opened the back door and there was a striped cat asking for something to eat.

No one who was hungry was ever turned away from Mr. Jack's restaurant. And so Mr. Jack put a dish of food and a dish of milk by the back door.

Before Mr. Jack went home that night he looked out of the back door of his restaurant. The striped cat was asleep in a box beside the door.

In the morning when Mr. Jack opened his restaurant, he looked out the back door.

The cat was in her box with three little kittens. She meowed and purred and showed Mr. Jack her three striped babies.

"I am going to call you Mary," said Mr. Jack. "Mary is my wife and she is just as proud of our three children as you are proud of your babies."

From that time, Mary lived in a box at the back door of Mr. Jack's restaurant. There was always a dish of food and a dish of milk for her.

Some of the dogs would have liked to eat the food. But Mary soon made them understand that they had to keep away from the back door of Mr. Jack's restaurant.

One morning Mr. Jack looked into the box to see the kittens. Now there were five kittens in the box. One was white and one was black.

"Mary, Mary," said Mr. Jack, "Where did you get that white kitten and that black kitten?"

Mary just meowed and purred. She closed her eyes and seemed to smile. But she did not tell Mr. Jack where she had found the white kitten and the black kitten.

"Mary," said Mr. Jack, "you will have to have a bigger box for a bigger family."

And now every day Mr. Jack put a bigger dish of food and a bigger dish of milk outside the back door of his restaurant.

Very soon Mary brought home a yellow kitten. Now there were six kittens in the big box and Mary was very happy.

There was always a dish of food and a dish of milk for the growing family.

Mary washed her kittens and took good care of them. And when the kittens grew big enough they got out of the box and played around the back door of Mr. Jack's restaurant.

Mary was very happy with her good home and her family of kittens. When the kittens got big they would go away.

Almost every day Mary would leave her kittens. When she came home she would be carrying another kitten in her mouth.

Nobody knew where Mary had found the kittens. But the kittens were always hungry.

The last time Mr. Jack counted the kittens, there were thirteen kittens in the big box beside the back door of his restaurant.

"Mary," said Mr. Jack, "I never thought I would be feeding so many kittens. But if you can take care of all those kittens, I guess I can feed them."

Mr. Jack put a bigger dish of food and a bigger dish of milk outside the back door of his restaurant.

And when Mary's babies got big enough to go away, she found more baby kittens and brought them to her big box beside Mr. Jack's back door.

Ho's Gifts

There are many stories about cats who bring gifts to their owners. Some cats bring a mouse and lay it at the feet of their mistress. Some cats bring a baby rabbit or a baby bird and ask their master to look after it.

One cat brought things to eat to his mistress. She never knew where the cat got the fish and the pieces of meat that he laid at her feet. The cat never ate any of the food.

Ho was a Siamese cat and he loved his Mistress very much. He liked to visit other houses in the neighborhood.

Whenever Ho saw something that he thought his Mistress would like, he took it in his mouth and carried it home. He brought her a glove. He brought her a stocking and a piece of ribbon.

Ho's Mistress was always trying to find the owners of the gifts that Ho brought her. She could not break the cat of the habit of taking things that belonged to other people. He thought his Mistress should like his presents.

One day Ho brought his Mistress a ball of yellow yarn. His Mistress knew that someone was knitting a sweater and would need the ball of yellow yarn to finish the sweater.

She could not find anyone in the neighborhood who was knitting a yellow sweater.

The next day Ho brought his Mistress a sleeve which was knitted from the yellow yarn.

She talked to Ho, but Ho could not tell her where he had found the sleeve made of yellow yarn.

Ho must have thought that his Mistress liked the yellow yarn.

The next day Ho came home with the rest of the yellow sweater which was still on the knitting needles.

The Mistress saw that the yarn was still tied to the sweater. The yarn went over her back fence and through the next yard.

The Mistress took the sweater and the sleeve and followed the yarn. She went through the next yard and down the street. She wondered how Ho had carried the sweater so far. She walked a long way and came to a backyard where she found the end of the yellow yarn.

The lady of the house said that she had been knitting the yellow sweater in the backyard. She had gone into the house to answer the telephone. She had forgotten that she had left the yellow sweater on a chair in the backyard.

The lady of the house laughed when she heard about Ho.

"Maybe my cat will stay at home if I knit a yellow sweater," said Ho's Mistress.

Rusty

Rusty was a beautiful orange colored cat. One day, with his bushy tail held high, he walked into a large hotel in New York City. Rusty lived in that hotel for fifteen years.

Everyone in the hotel loved Rusty and looked after him. Mr. Case, the owner of the hotel, lived in an apartment on the tenth floor. This was "home" to Rusty.

Rusty rode up and down in the elevator. He knew when the elevator came to the tenth floor. He got out of the elevator and walked down the long hall. Then he meowed at the door of Mr. Case's apartment. Rusty never made a mistake.

Coming down in the elevator, Rusty sometimes stopped at the fourth floor. On the fourth floor lived a man who understood cats. This man had made friends with Rusty. He always had a bit of fish or a piece of meat for Rusty. And Rusty would call at his door very often.

Only once did Rusty ever get off the elevator at any floor except the tenth floor and the fourth floor.

One day Rusty had gone down to the lobby of the hotel. He liked to watch the people. And he liked to sleep in one of the soft chairs.

A French poodle came into the hotel lobby with his Mistress. This French poodle hated cats. As soon as he came into the lobby, he smelled a cat. He was such a strong dog that his Mistress could not hold him on the leash.

Before anyone knew what had happened, the big French poodle had Rusty in his mouth and was shaking the life out of him.

Everyone in the lobby was running around and making a great noise. But no one could make the big French poodle let go of Rusty.

Then a man poured a pitcher of water on the nose of the dog. The big dog had to open his mouth to get some air. Rusty ran for his life.

The door to one of the elevators was open. Rusty dashed into the elevator.

The elevator boy shut the door and took Rusty up to the tenth floor.

But this time Rusty did not get off at the tenth floor. He just sat in the back of the elevator with big frightened eyes.

Rusty did not get out of the elevator until it came to the highest floor. Then the cat got out and ran up some stairs to the roof of the hotel.

Rusty stayed on the roof of the hotel for four days. Then he got hungry and came down to his "home" on the tenth floor.

Charles

Charles was a Siamese cat. Charles made a lot of noise, for his purr was like the noise of an engine. And he meowed in a loud voice as many Siamese cats do. But Charles was very smart.

When Charles was a kitten he wanted to learn everything at once. He ran all over the house. He knocked things down. And his Master had to put all his pretty vases away in the cupboard.

Charles climbed the curtains and his sharp claws tore them. But the Master only laughed and said, "Charles, you will have to grow up and be a good cat."

Charles thought the running water in the bathroom was very funny. He watched it with big blue eyes, but he did not want any water to get on him.

There were two things that Charles hated very much. One was the vacuum cleaner which made such a funny noise. Charles would run and hide under the bed whenever he heard the vacuum cleaner.

But most of all, Charles hated firecrackers. He was always surprised at what a loud noise those little things made.

Charles was much interested in Rupert, the canary. Rupert lived in a cage. The cage hung on a stand. Charles would sit and look up at Rupert. He wanted to get nearer to the bird. Day after day, he jumped at Rupert's cage. But he could not get near the canary.

One day, Charles gave a big jump and hit the stand. Over went the stand and the cage fell down to the floor.

Charles sat on the floor beside the cage and looked at Rupert.

Charles did not try to hurt the canary in any way. After that Rupert's cage was hung where Charles could not get at it.

Charles never again showed any interest in birds. Even when he played outdoors, he never tried to catch a bird.

Charles was a gentle cat and did not want to fight other cats. Once a big tomcat bit off the end of Charles's tail. Charles would not fight. He ran to his Master.

Even if Charles would not fight, he was a very brave cat.

Although Charles hated noise, he went to war with his Master. He rode in airplanes and on trains and in automobiles and trucks. He went from camp to camp. The soldiers loved him and gave him good things to eat.

His Master became ill and had to go to the hospital. Charles went to the hospital too. He stayed with his Master and helped him to get well.

Charles lived to be a very old cat. He liked to sleep in the sun. He did not want to play with the younger cats. One day Charles went to sleep and did not wake up.

Purrikens

Mrs. Wright was a little old lady who lived by herself with her cat Purrikens. Purrikens was a big black cat and a very smart cat.

Purrikens knew just what time Mrs. Wright wanted to get up in the morning. He would jump on her bed and pat her face with his paw until she opened her eyes.

Mrs. Wright said that Purrikens woke her each morning at the same time. She wondered how the cat knew the time.

But one time in the middle of the night Purrikens jumped on Mrs. Wright's bed and patted her face with his paw. Mrs. Wright pushed Purrikens off the bed.

"It is not morning, Purrikens. It is the middle of the night. Go to sleep and leave me alone."

Purrikens jumped right up on the bed again. He meowed and meowed in such a strange way that Mrs. Wright got out of bed.

"What is the matter, Purrikens? Do you want to go out of doors?"

Mrs. Wright was very sleepy but she got up and turned on the light.

Purrikens ran to the door and looked back at Mrs. Wright and meowed in that strange way.

"All right, Purrikens," said Mrs. Wright as she put on her dressing gown. "I will let you go out of doors."

Then Mrs. Wright heard someone calling her name. And someone was pounding on the front door.

Mrs. Wright knew that something was the matter. She hurried into the living room. As soon as she went into the living room, she smelled smoke. The house was on fire.

Mrs. Wright opened the front door, and the neighbor said, "Thank goodness you are awake. I have called the firemen. They will be here right away."

Mrs. Wright with Purrikens in her arms ran to a neighbor.

The firemen came at once and saved the little house.

"Purrikens saved my life," said Mrs. Wright. "I was sound asleep. I am afraid the house would have burned down and I would have burned to death if Purrikens had not jumped on my bed and patted my face."

Mrs. Wright wrote a letter to the newspaper telling how Purrikens had saved her life. And the newspaper printed the letter.

The people from all over town came to the little house to see Purrikens. They called him a hero.

Mrs. Wright and Purrikens lived together a long time. And every morning the big black cat woke his dear Mistress at the same time. He jumped on her bed and patted her face with his paw until she opened her eyes.

Puddles Was a Fisherman

All cats like to eat fish. But few cats go out and catch their own fish.

There was a cat in Florida who lived in a small hotel by the ocean. Men from the city stayed at this hotel so that they could go fishing out on the pier that was built out into the ocean.

Every morning this big gray cat followed a fisherman out to the pier. He would sit beside the fisherman and wait until the man caught a fish.

51

As soon as the fish was taken off the hook, the cat would take it in his mouth. The big gray cat would run to the cook at the hotel. And the cook always cooked the fish and gave it to the cat.

The fishermen said that the cat brought them good luck. They always caught fish when the big gray cat came to the pier. The cat seemed to know which man would catch the first fish.

Then the big gray cat became a fisherman. His Master, who earned his living as a fisherman, told the story.

"When Puddles was a little kitten, he had fleas. I took him down to the ocean and gave him a bath. He liked the water so much that he went every day for a swim in the ocean.

"I started taking Puddles out with me in my fishing boat. When Puddles was with me I always thought I caught more fish.

"I taught Puddles to be a good cat on the boat," said the fisherman. "He never touched one of the fish that I caught unless I gave it to him. But he would stand in front of the boat and look down into the water.

"One day I ran into a school of fish. There were fish all around the boat. Suddenly Puddles, who was a good swimmer, jumped into the water. He caught a fish in his mouth.

"Puddles certainly looked funny. He was swimming as hard as he could swim and carrying the fish in his mouth.

"I pulled Puddles into the boat. And from that time he has caught his own fish. But I have always said the big gray cat brought me good luck."

Puddles has lived to be a very old cat.

The men from the city still try to get Puddles to go out on the pier with them. They think that they will catch many fish if Puddles sits beside them.

Sometimes Puddles is lazy and he lets the fishermen from the city catch his fish.

Grandmother's Chair

Grandmother liked to sit by the window in a little rocking chair. No one else in the family ever sat in this chair.

"It is Grandmother's chair," said Tom.

"It is Grandmother's chair," said Mary.

But Tiger, the big striped cat thought Grandmother's chair was his chair.

Every time Tiger came into the house, he looked to see if Grandmother was sitting in her chair. If Grandmother was not sitting in her chair, Tiger jumped into the rocking chair and went to sleep.

"Look at Tiger," said Tom. "He is asleep in Grandmother's rocking chair."

But Grandmother would laugh when she saw Tiger asleep in her chair.

"You look so comfortable, Tiger," said Grandmother. "I will sit in another chair until you have had your nap."

One day Grandmother was sitting in her rocking chair when Tiger came into the room.

Tiger looked at Grandmother a long time. Grandmother was reading a book and did not look at Tiger.

Tiger walked all around Grandmother's chair and meowed. Tiger could not get Grandmother to understand that he wanted to go to sleep in her rocking chair.

Then the big cat laid down at her feet and went to sleep.

And Grandmother went on reading her book.

Tiger opened his eyes and looked at Grandmother. Sleeping on the floor was not as nice as sleeping in Grandmother's chair.

Tiger went to the door and meowed and meowed.

"All right," said Grandmother, putting down her book. "You are a good cat and always ask to go outdoors. I will let you go out."

Grandmother went to the door and opened it, but Tiger did not go out doors. He turned and ran and jumped into Grandmother's rocking chair. He shut his eyes as if he were sound asleep.

Grandmother laughed and laughed. She called Tom and Mary and told them how Tiger had fooled her.

"Tiger is a smart cat," said Grandmother. "I think I will let him have his nap in my rocking chair."

Pansy

Pansy lived in a big city. Even as a kitten, Pansy liked to walk the streets of the city.

Pansy learned how to keep away from people's feet. She learned how to cross streets and not get run over by automobiles. But when evening came, Pansy always came home for supper. She was always hungry.

Pansy grew to be a very beautiful cat. She still walked the streets of the big city. Her master, Mr. Joseph, was always afraid that something would happen to Pansy. City streets are no place for a beautiful cat.

One evening Pansy did not come home at suppertime. Mr. Joseph called and called, but no Pansy came.

The next day Pansy did not come home. Mr. Joseph called and called, but no Pansy came. He was sure that something had happened to Pansy. Mr. Joseph was sad, for he loved his cat.

Mr. Joseph went to a printer and had a handbill printed. It said that Pansy was a beautiful black and white cat. She was lost. Mr. Joseph would give a reward to anyone who brought Pansy home.

He put the handbills up on fences and walls.

That evening a little boy came to the door. He told Mr. Joseph that he had seen Pansy hiding in a back yard.

It was getting dark, so Mr. Joseph got a flashlight. He went with the little boy for he was afraid Pansy might be hurt.

Mr. Joseph and the little boy climbed over many fences. They went in many back yards. At last they found a little cat hiding in a box. But the cat was not Pansy.

Mr. Joseph gave the boy a quarter and thanked him for telling him about the cat that was hiding in the back yard.

The next morning two little boys came to the door. One little boy carried a black cat and one little boy carried a white cat.

"Which cat is Pansy?" asked the boys.

"No, no," said Mr. Joseph. "Pansy is a black and white cat."

Mr. Joseph said, "Thank you for trying to find Pansy for me." He gave each of the boys a quarter.

The next boy that came to the door had a yellow cat.

"Is this cat Pansy?" asked the boy.

"No, No," said Mr. Joseph. "The handbill said that Pansy was a black and white cat."

But he gave the boy a quarter.

The word had gotten around that Mr. Joseph would give a quarter if a boy brought a cat to his door. And the boys could always find a cat.

The boys thought this was an easy way to earn a quarter.

One boy told another boy how he could earn a quarter.

All day long boys came with cats. There were little cats and big cats. There were gray cats and striped cats. There were young cats and old cats. There were black cats and white cats.

But no boy brought back Pansy. Mr. Joseph did not know what to do. At last he had to stop giving the boys a quarter when they brought a cat to his door.

Mr. Joseph was sure that he would never see Pansy again.

She must have been killed on the streets of the big city.

One evening about a week later, Pansy came home for supper. She never told Mr. Joseph where she had been.

Mr. Joseph laughed when he saw Pansy.

"You pretty cat," said Mr. Joseph. "I am glad you came home. But you certainly cost me a lot of quarters."

Minnie and Matt

Minnie and Matt lived with Mrs. Jones. Minnie was a mother cat with three babies. The mother cat had a box under the kitchen table where her babies had a nice warm bed.

Matt was a dog. He and Minnie were good friends. Every day Matt came into the kitchen and looked into the box where the kittens slept. He never tried to hurt the kittens for Matt was a kind dog.

The three kittens had just opened their eyes. They began to crawl around in their box. Minnie knew it was time for her kittens to have a new place to sleep.

The mother cat went all over the house. She went to the living room and jumped up in a chair that was nice and soft. Minnie thought the chair would be a nice place for her babies.

Mrs. Jones came into the room.

"Hello Minnie," said Mrs. Jones. "I am going to sit down in that chair."

Minnie knew that this was no place for her babies.

Minnie went into the bedroom. She jumped up on the bed. This was a nice soft place for her kittens. Minnie was a little cat. She looked over the side of the bed. The floor was far below her. This would never do. Her little babies would fall off the bed and get hurt.

Minnie jumped off the bed. She went all around the bedroom. At last she came to the closet. And the closet door was open. Minnie went in the closet.

There in the dark, warm closet was a soft rug in a corner. This was just the place for her babies.

Minnie went back to her box in the kitchen. The kittens were hungry.

After Minnie had fed her babies, she took one kitten in her mouth. She got the kitten out of the box. She tried to carry it across the kitchen floor.

But Minnie was a little cat. The kitten was too big for her to carry it as mother cats carry their babies. Minnie did not know what to do. She sat beside her kitten a long time.

At last Minnie went to find Matt. The dog was asleep under the dining room table.

Somehow Minnie told Matt that she was in trouble. She wanted him to come to the kitchen. The dog and the cat went to the kitchen. Minnie sat down beside her little kitten that was on the kitchen floor.

The mother cat took the kitten in her mouth and showed Matt how to carry it. She pushed the kitten toward Matt. He did not understand.

Minnie took Matt to the bedroom. She showed him the nice soft rug in the closet. She tried to tell Matt that this rug would be a bed for her kittens.

Minnie and Matt went back to the kitchen. Again Minnie took the kitten in her mouth and showed Matt how to carry it. This time Matt understood. He took the kitten in his mouth. He was careful not to hurt it.

Minnie ran to the bedroom. This time Matt understood. He carefully carried the kitten into the bedroom and put it on the soft rug in the closet.

One at a time, the kind dog carried the kittens into the bedroom and put them in the closet.

Minnie was very happy in her new home.

As the kittens grew bigger, Minnie would want another place for her family. She always went and got Matt. Matt understood. He would take a kitten in his mouth and carry it to whatever place Minnie had picked out for her family.

When all three kittens were in the new place, Matt would sit beside Minnie and wag his tail.

Perhaps Matt was saying "See what a smart dog I am. I can look after baby kittens too."

That Kitten

Mai Ling is a Siamese kitten. She is pretty. She is cute. And Mai Ling is smart. Since she came to live with Mr. Davis, Mai Ling runs the house.

All Siamese cats like to climb. And Mai Ling will climb anything. She climbs up people's legs to get to their laps. She leaves silk stockings full of runs.

Mai Ling climbs up curtains. When she gets to the ceiling, the kitten gets afraid. She hangs on with all claws out. And she tears the curtain from top to bottom.

Mr. Davis has a dog named Hero. Hero thought he would run Mai out of the house.

Hero is twenty times as big as Mai Ling. He acted very fierce as if he was going to hurt the kitten. But Mai Ling faced Hero. She jumped at his nose with all her claws out. Now it is Hero who runs away and hides.

Mai Ling hunts Hero all over the house. When she finds him asleep in the corner, the kitten jumps on his head. Before Hero knows what has happened, Mai Ling has run away and gone under the sofa where Hero cannot reach her. If Hero should put his head under the sofa to see if Mai Ling was there, the kitten's claws would be in his nose.

At night, Mai Ling wakes up and jumps on the bed where Mr. Davis is sleeping. If he moves, Mai Ling plays she has found a mouse. Mr. Davis has to stay very still.

Mai Ling will purr like a little engine. And if Mr. Davis is very, very quiet Mai Ling will go to sleep.

The room that Mai Ling likes best is the bathroom. She cannot understand how the water comes out of the faucet. She puts her paw into the water.

One of the most interesting things in her life is to watch Mr. Davis shave each morning. She sits on the edge of the tub and watches him with her big blue eyes.

In the bathroom, Mai Ling finds many things to climb.

One morning while Mr. Davis was shaving, Mai Ling started up the window curtain. The kitten went up until she reached the ceiling. Mai Ling looked down. The white tub was under her. It was a long way down.

Mai Ling was afraid. She cried and cried. Mr. Davis went on with his shaving. Mai Ling tried to turn around. But her claws which had helped her climb up the window curtain did not help her climb down the window curtain.

By now, Mai Ling was very much afraid. She cried and cried.

Mai Ling cried out in such a loud voice that Mrs. Davis came running to see what was the matter.

"Mai Ling, come down from that window curtain," said Mrs. Davis.

The kitten gave a big jump and landed on the shower curtain.

Now shower curtains are not made for kitten's claws. The shower curtain was torn as Mai Ling slid down to the white tub.

Mrs. Davis picked Mai Ling up and said, "Pretty soon Mai Ling will grow up to be a mother cat. Then she will not tear shower curtains to pieces."

As Mr. Davis finished shaving, he said to himself, "Mai Ling will be a mother cat and have five little kittens. They will be as pretty and as cute and as smart as Mai Ling.

"What will Hero and I do?"

The Cat Dance

Once there was a beautiful dancer who was afraid of cats. When she was a little girl, she had played with a cat. She hurt the cat and the cat had scratched her. After that, she was afraid of all cats.

When the little girl, whose name was Fanny, grew up she became a famous ballet dancer. She was asked to dance in a ballet where she was supposed to be a white cat.

The story of the ballet was about a Chinese Princess who fell in love with a Prince who loved cats. He would not look at the beautiful Princess. He loved his cats more than anybody in the world.

The Princess went to a Man of Magic and asked him how she could win the love of the Prince.

The Man of Magic changed the Princess into a white cat. The Prince thought the White Cat was the most beautiful white cat that he had ever seen.

The White Cat was loving and gentle. He loved her very much.

The Man of Magic did not want the Prince to love a cat more than the Princess.

But then the White Cat began to do all the naughty things a cat can do. It spit at the Prince. It scratched the Prince. Pretty soon the Prince hated the White Cat. He began to hate all cats.

The Man of Magic turned the White Cat back into the beautiful Princess. The Prince fell in love with her and they were married.

That is the story of the ballet that was danced to very beautiful music. Throughout the dance, Fanny had to act like a cat.

It you have watched a cat, you know how beautifully a cat moves. The cat walks with tail held high when it is happy. The cat rubs against those it loves and purrs. When the cat is angry it puts up its back. It spits and scratches. When the cat plays with a ball, it jumps high and hits the ball with its paws.

Fanny wanted the movements of her dance to be like the movements of a cat.

"I had to buy a white cat," said Fanny. "I went to a pet shop and got a little white kitten."

Although Fanny was afraid every time she put her hand on that white kitten, she took it home. The white kitten was loving and gentle. It loved Fanny and played around the house.

Fanny watched the kitten and tried to do just what the kitten did.

As the kitten grew to be a cat, Fanny lost her fear of cats. She learned to act just like a cat. She learned to try and catch a mouse just like a cat. She learned to play with a ball. She learned to sleep all curled up just like a cat.

It was the night of the ballet. The theater lights were dim. Beautiful music was heard. The curtain went up.

The stage was a beautiful Chinese garden. The Princess was there on the stage and the Man of Magic. They danced together. Slowly the Princess was turned into a White Cat.

The White Cat stretched and ran about the stage. It rubbed against the Man of Magic to show how happy it was.

When the Prince came on the stage, you knew the Prince would love this beautiful White Cat.

But the naughty White Cat went very wild. It spit at the Prince and scratched him. The Prince hated the White Cat.

Then the Man of Magic turned the White Cat back into the Princess. And everybody was happy.

Fanny danced a beautiful Cat Dance. When the curtain came down, the audience clapped and clapped. Fanny came before the curtain with her white cat in her arms. She bowed to the audience.

Firehouse No. 6

All was quiet in Firehouse No. 6. It was a hot day and the big doors were open. Some of the men were playing cards. Some of the men were taking a nap. And the pet bulldog, Red, was asleep in his box.

At this time Sam thought he would visit Firehouse No. 6. Sam was a big striped cat. He was a proud cat and he walked with his tail held high.

Sam rubbed against the legs of two men sitting by the door. Sam purred and said meow. The men laughed and one man said, "You can come in and look around, but Red will soon chase you out."

Sam walked into Firehouse No. 6. The big cat climbed up on the engine. It smelled different and Sam liked the smell.

Pretty soon Sam climbed down from the fire engine. He went up some stairs to the place where the firemen slept. Then Sam went to sleep on one of the beds.

Red, the bulldog, was still asleep. All that hot afternoon Sam, the striped cat, slept on the bed of one of the firemen. And Red, the bulldog, slept in his box.

Slowly Red opened his eyes. Then suddenly he was wide awake. Red smelled a cat. He jumped out of his box. That cat had been walking around his firehouse. That cat had been on his fire engine. That cat had walked up the stairs and slept in a bed.

Red did not want a cat in Firehouse No. 6. He was going to get that cat and kill it.

In the firehouse there is a big brass pole that goes from the upstairs to the downstairs. When the fire alarm rings, the men who are upstairs slide down the pole. It is the quickest way for them to get downstairs and onto the fire engine.

This pole was right beside the bed where Sam was sleeping.

Sam woke up with a start. He saw a big bulldog that was about to get him. There was only one way that the cat could get away from the dog.

Sam jumped for the brass pole. This pole was not like a tree.

Sam could not hold on to the pole with his claws. Sam put his paws around the pole and held on. He slid down the pole just like a fireman.

Sam could hear Red growling. As soon as Sam hit the floor he ran to the fire engine. He jumped up on the seat where the big dog could not get him.

Some of the firemen had seen Sam slide down the pole. They were laughing and telling the other firemen how the cat had gotten away from Red because a dog could not slide down the brass pole.

The firemen said that such a smart cat that could get away from Red could stay in Firehouse No. 6.

Sam had learned two things. One: a dog cannot slide down a brass pole. Two: a smart cat can slide down a brass pole and it is a lot of fun.

From that day, Sam has lived at Firehouse No. 6. He likes to sleep on the fireman's bed that is nearest to the brass pole. Whenever the fire alarm rings, Sam is the first one to slide down the pole. He sits on the engine and goes to the fire.

Red has become an old dog.
He lives in the country now.
He sleeps in the sun.

Sometimes he may dream of
Firehouse No. 6. He may dream
of Sam, the cat he could never
catch.

The Love of David

David was a black kitten. He was so black that when he closed his eyes he was as black as midnight. He got his blue eyes from his Siamese mother. But his father must have been a very black cat.

David came to live in a house with two big cats. One cat was brown and white and was called Rabbit. The other cat was a very big gray cat and was called Heathcliff.

The two big cats would have nothing to do with David. When David wanted to play, the big cats would go outdoors and hide under the bushes.

One day David was very brave. He went outdoors too. Heathcliff saw him and chased him under a doghouse that was in the back yard. The doghouse was set up on blocks. There was just enough room for the black kitten to crawl under it.

David stayed under the dog house. And Heathcliff walked around and around the dog house.

At last the big gray cat went away and sat on the grass looking at the doghouse. He seemed to say, "Black kitten, you do as I tell you to do, or I will not let you come out from under the doghouse."

Slowly David crawled out from under the doghouse. He went over to the big gray cat and touched his nose.

From that day on, Heathcliff was David's friend. Wherever Heathcliff went, David followed.

The big cat taught David everything that a kitten should know.

Heathcliff taught David bird watching and mouse catching. He taught him how to fight and how to hide from danger. He even let David sleep with him in his basket.

Even Rabbit became David's friend. The brown and white cat sometimes let David play with his tail. But it was the big gray cat that David loved best.

Heathcliff and David ate together and played together. They played together all over the house and yard. Heathcliff even washed David as a mother cat washes her kitten.

David was a happy little kitten.

One day Heathcliff went out on the road. He did not see the car that was coming so fast. The car hit Heathcliff. He was taken to a doctor, but the doctor could not save him.

David hunted all over the house. He cried and called to his friend. But Heathcliff did not come. Then David hunted all over the yard and Rabbit hunted with him. They could not find Heathcliff.

For a long week the brown and white cat and the black kitten hunted for their friend. But they could not find him.

At last Rabbit understood that Heathcliff was gone. Rabbit must have been sorry for the black kitten for he began to wash David's fur and play with him.

David grew to be a big cat. And sometimes he would hunt in the house and in the yard as if he were hunting for Heathcliff.

David made friends with all the other cats in the neighborhood. There was a broken window in the cellar. Every night the cats came through the broken window and visited with David.

But David never forgot

Heathcliff. One evening he brought a big gray cat into the living room. He showed the big gray cat the box of toys that he and Heathcliff used to play with.

But the big gray cat did not know how to play with a ball or a piece of string or a catnip mouse. This big gray cat was not Heathcliff.

The big gray cat ran down into the cellar and out the broken window. David followed him into the cellar and sat by the broken window all night.

One day Joe Bulldozer came into the kitchen carrying something in his mouth as a mother cat carries a kitten.

Very carefully, Joe laid a baby rabbit at the feet of the Man-of-the-House. Joe went out again and carried in another baby rabbit.

The Man-of-the-House put the baby rabbits into a little box and carried them out into the garden. He hoped that the mother rabbit would find them and take care of them.

Joe never tried to hurt any little animals.

Joe made friends with all the neighbors. That is, the neighbors who liked cats. He seemed to know when anyone was going to have a party. Joe always liked to go to a party for he liked cake very much.

Once Joe was hit by a car. He crawled under some bushes. The Man-of-the-House found him and took him to a doctor. He was a very sick cat and almost died. But Joe Bulldozer got well.

Then Joe went to the city. He lived in an apartment. Joe visited all the other apartments.

Everybody loved the beautiful yellow cat. One day the Lady-of-the-House brought home a black kitten. Joe would not stay at home with a black kitten. He bulldozed his way into another apartment where there were no kittens.

Sometimes Joe goes calling on the Lady-of-the-House. She will give him a piece of cake. And Joe will purr his loud, loud purr. When the yellow cat has finished his cake, he will ask to be let out. Then Joe Bulldozer goes to his new home.

Tomcat

Farmer Brown thought that Tomcat was the ugliest cat that he had ever seen. Tomcat was long and thin and black. He had been in so many fights that pieces of his fur had been torn away. His ears had been chewed. And one eye was almost closed because another cat had scratched him in the face.

Tomcat lived in Farmer Brown's barn. He caught the rats and mice that wanted to eat the corn.

Farmer Brown milked the cows morning and night. He always left a dish of milk in the barn for Tomcat.

Farmer Brown carried the milk into the house. Just the horses and cows were left in the barn. Then Tomcat would come out from his hiding place.

Tomcat was afraid of people. He would look all around to see that no one was in the barn. Then he would drink his milk.

No one had ever petted Tomcat. And I think no one had ever heard Tomcat purr.

Mrs. Brown's sister lived on a farm about three miles away.

One day the sister came to see Mrs. Brown. She brought her beautiful cat Molly with her.

"I will have to go away from home for about three weeks," said Mrs. Brown's sister. "I am afraid to leave Molly at home. She is going to have kittens very soon."

"I will take very good care of Molly," said Mrs. Brown. "When you get home, I will bring her to you."

"Molly's kittens will be born any day," said the sister.

"We must fix Molly a box in the kitchen so that she will have a nice home for her family," said Mrs. Brown.

But Molly did not like the box in the kitchen. She went out into the barn. She made herself a nest in the hay. And she met Tomcat.

Molly loved Tomcat as soon as she saw him. She rubbed against Tomcat and purred.

For the first time in Tomcat's life another cat loved him. Tomcat was very happy. He caught mice and brought them to Molly. And now Farmer Brown left two dishes of milk.

In two days Molly's kittens were born. Tomcat sat beside the nest and watched over Molly. If anyone came into the barn, he would spit and growl. He was going to look after Molly.

When the kittens were a week old, Molly let Farmer Brown and Mrs. Brown see that she had three kittens. Mrs. Brown carried the kittens into the house and put them in the box in the kitchen.

But Molly did not like the box in the kitchen. One by one the mother cat carried her kittens back to the barn and put them in her nest in the hay.

When the kittens were three weeks old, Mrs. Brown put Molly and her kittens in the car and took them to her sister's farm.

Molly stayed at the farm just one night.

The next afternoon Mrs. Brown saw Molly coming down the road carrying a kitten in her mouth. She was very tired and could hardly walk.

Molly had walked over three miles and carried a kitten all the way.

Molly took the kitten to the barn and put it in her nest in the hay.

Mrs. Brown watched. Pretty soon she saw Molly and Tomcat come out of the barn. They walked down the road together.

Early the next morning when Farmer Brown went to the barn to milk the cows, he saw Molly and Tomcat coming down the road.

Each cat was carrying a kitten in its mouth. The two cats were very tired. All night long they had been walking down the road.

They carried the kittens into the barn and put them in the nest in the hay.

Now Molly and Tomcat were happy again.

Tomcat would sit by the nest and watch the kittens while Molly went to the house. He would not let the kittens get out of the nest. Sometimes Molly would take the kittens into the house to show them to Mrs. Brown.

When her sister came back from the city, Mrs. Brown told her the story of Molly and Tomcat.

Then her sister said, "I have not the heart to take Molly away from Tomcat. I will let you keep Molly. When the kittens are bigger, I will take them home."

"Now I have a family of cats in my barn," said Farmer Brown.

Molly and Tomcat went on living in Farmer Brown's barn. Every day Tomcat caught a mouse and brought it to Molly. And every day Farmer Brown left two dishes of milk in the barn for the two cats.

Mother Cat

Most mother cats look after their kittens and keep them from harm. There are stories of mother cats going into burning houses to get their kittens.

Lon Hai was a Siamese cat. She was a very beautiful cat and had won many ribbons at cat shows.

Lon Hai was out in the yard with her Mistress. She always went walking on a leash like a dog. But this day Lon Hai slipped out of her collar and ran up a tree.

Lon Hai did not come down when her Mistress called. She kept going higher up in the tree.

Then Lon Hai looked down at her Mistress. Never had the little cat been so frightened.

She held on to the tree with her sharp claws. She cried and cried as only a Siamese cat can cry. She was so frightened that she could not move.

Lon Hai's Mistress went and got the Master. He went to a neighbor and got a very long ladder. He put the ladder up against the tree. He climbed up and got Lon Hai out of the tree.

Lon Hai was still so frightened that she could not walk. She just lay on the ground and looked at her Mistress with big blue eyes that seemed to say, "I will never climb a tree again."

When Lon Hai had her first kittens, she was a good mother. Lon Hai took good care of her kittens. They all looked as if they were going to grow up to be as beautiful as their mother.

All the kittens but one went to new homes. This little kitten was going to be sent a long way. It should grow to be a bigger kitten before it was sent to its new home.

Lon Hai had such good times with her little kitten. She washed her many times a day and kept her as white as snow. She played games with the kitten all over the house.

One day the Mistress thought that Lon Hai should take a walk in the yard. She got the leash and she and Lon Hai went for a walk. They did not take the kitten.

The kitten cried and cried. The Mistress felt very sorry for the kitten.

"Poor little kitten," said the Mistress. "Do you want to go out doors?"

She went back into the house
and took the kitten in her arms.
She carried it out doors with Lon
Hai walking beside her on the
leash.

But as soon as the kitten was
out doors, it jumped down to the
grass. Away it went before the
Mistress could catch it. The kitten
climbed up a tree. The little
kitten went up, up, up.

The Mistress stood at the bottom
of the tree and called and called.

The little kitten looked down.
Then it became so frightened that
it could not move. The kitten
cried and cried.

Lon Hai called to her kitten. But the kitten just cried and cried.

Then the Mistress sat on the ground and took Lon Hai in her lap. She talked to the mother cat a long time.

"Lon Hai, listen to me very carefully. The Master is not home. He cannot go and get the long ladder and get your kitten out of the tree.

"Lon Hai, you are the only one that can get your kitten to come down from the tree."

The Mistress took the leash off Lon Hai and put her up in the tree. The cat understood.

Lon Hai began to climb the tree. Very slowly she went up, up, up, to where her kitten was crying.

The Mistress could hear the Siamese cat talking to her kitten. Pretty soon the kitten stopped crying.

Then very slowly Lon Hai began to go backward down the tree.

She was showing her little kitten how to come down from a tree. Very slowly the kitten began to back down the tree.

The little kitten would get frightened and stop. Then Lon Hai would have to talk to her kitten again.

Lon Hai took a long time to get her kitten to back down the tree for the kitten was very frightened and would stop and cry.

The Mistress stood at the bottom of the tree. She did not say a word for she knew that she could not help.

Lon Hai was very frightened but the Mistress knew that she would try to save her kitten.

At last the Mistress could reach the mother cat and her kitten. She took them into her arms and carried them into the house.

The poor little mother cat was so weak with fright that she could not stand. It was the kitten who washed the mother cat's face.

I think that the kitten was thanking her mother for getting her down from that awful tree.

Kathleen's Christmas Present

Robert kept thinking of Kathleen. He was sorry for her. She was a little girl with no brothers and sisters. She lived in the city and she had no one to play with.

Kathleen and her mother had spent the summer on the farm where Robert lived.

When Kathleen came she was thin and white. She had been very sick. But on the farm, Kathleen began to feel better. Soon she was laughing and playing with Robert.

Robert and Kathleen played with Shep, the dog who took the sheep to the pasture. They helped Robert's mother gather the eggs each day. They played in the barn and watched Robert's father milk the cows.

One day Robert and Kathleen found Tabbie with four little kittens in a nest in the barn.

Kathleen had never seen any baby kittens. She ran to her mother.

"Oh, Mother, Mother!" Kathleen cried. "Tabbie has four babies, and they are so little their eyes are shut."

All summer Kathleen watched the kittens grow.

Now she would rather play with the kittens than play with Shep the dog. She would rather play with the kittens than watch Robert's father milk the cows. It was a happy summer for Kathleen.

Kathleen and her mother had to go back to the city. Kathleen cried because she did not want to leave the kittens.

Robert would have liked to give Kathleen one of the kittens. But her mother said that the city was so far away that she could not take the kitten with her.

Robert watched the kittens playing in the barn. They were almost big cats now. Tabbie was teaching them to catch the mice in the barn. It was getting cold and the mice were coming into the barn from the field.

Robert kept thinking of Kathleen. She must be lonesome for she had no one to play with. She would be happy with a kitten.

Then Robert had a wonderful thought. He would give Kathleen a kitten for a Christmas present.

"Mother," said Robert. "How can I give Kathleen one of my kittens for a Christmas present?"

"Kathleen lives in a big city," said mother. "The city is far away from our farm. It would cost a lot of money to send a kitten as a present for it would have to go by airplane."

"There must be kittens in a big city," said Robert. "How can I get one for Kathleen?"

"Father will know what to do," said mother. "Let us ask him how you can get a kitten for Kathleen."

Robert ran out to the barn where father was milking the cows.

"Father," said Robert. "How can I get a kitten for Kathleen?"

"Kathleen lives in a big city far away," said the father.

"There must be kittens in a big city," said Robert. "How can I get one for Kathleen?"

"In a big city there are many policemen," said father. "Policemen look after children and are kind to them. I think that a policeman might get a kitten for Kathleen."

"You might write a letter to the policemen of the city and ask if one of them could get a kitten for a little lonesome girl. And I will give you a five dollar bill to put in the letter."

Robert wrote a letter to the policemen in the big city.

Dear Policeman

I know a little girl named Kathleen. She lives at 1523 Grand Avenue. She is lonesome, for she has no one to play with.

I am putting five dollars in the letter. Please get Kathleen a pretty kitten for a Christmas present.

Your friend,
Robert

P.S. Please put a red ribbon on the kitten.

One day, just before Christmas, a policeman came to Kathleen's house. He carried a box with holes cut in it. There was something in the box that meowed.

"Does a little girl named Kathleen live here?" asked the policeman. "I have a Christmas present for her from a little boy named Robert."

The policeman opened the box and took out a pretty kitten with a red ribbon on it.

"Robert told Santa Claus to give you a pretty kitten to play with," said the policeman.

"Oh, oh, oh," cried Kathleen, as she took the kitten in her arms. "I never knew Santa Claus could be a policeman."

The Cowboy's Cat

One noon, the cowboys were sitting around in the shade of the bunk house. Suddenly a little black kitten walked up to one of the men.

The kitten was very thin and very tired, as if it had come a long way. Nobody knew where the kitten had come from, for there was not another house for ten miles.

"A black cat is good luck," said Jimmie, one of the cowboys.

"A black cat is bad luck," said another cowboy. "Mrs. Jones will never let a black cat stay on the ranch."

"The little kitten is hungry," said Jimmie. "I am sure that Mrs. Jones will give it some milk."

Jimmie took the little black kitten over to the kitchen where Mrs. Jones cooked for the cowboys. Mrs. Jones was a big woman and she did not like cats.

But the kitten was so little and so thin that she said she would give it some milk.

"It can stay in my kitchen for a few days," said Mrs. Jones. "And then you must take that cat away."

"Mrs. Jones," said Jimmie, "don't you know that a black cat brings good luck?"

"I don't believe in such nonsense," said Mrs. Jones.

But she let the kitten stay in her kitchen. The kitten stayed in a corner of the kitchen where Jimmie had fixed a box for her. She did not get in anybody's way.

The little black kitten grew to be a black cat without a bit of white on her.

All the cowboys loved Cat. They said that Cat brought good luck to the ranch.

Mrs. Jones still scolded. Every week she told the cowboys that Cat must go because she never had liked cats.

Then Cat would catch a mouse in the kitchen. And Mrs. Jones would say that Cat could stay a little longer.

One day Cat went away from the ranch. The cowboys hunted for her, but they could not find Cat. No one knew where Cat had gone. Cat was gone a whole week.

One morning, the cowboys found Cat asleep in her box in a corner of the kitchen. The cowboys were very happy to see their pet again.

"Good luck has come back to the ranch," said Jimmie.

"Bad luck is what I call that cat," said Mrs. Jones. But she let Cat stay in her kitchen.

One morning Cat did not get out of her box. That evening when the cowboys came in for supper, they looked in Cat's box. And Cat had four little black kittens.

Cat meowed as much as to say, "See my pretty babies."

Mrs. Jones said, "One cat is bad enough. But I will not have five cats in my kitchen. That cat and her kittens must go."

The cowboys were very sad. They knew that they must take Cat and her kittens away.

A man and his wife had a ranch on the other side of the river. It was ten miles away.

Jimmie said, "I think that Mrs. McDonald would like to have Cat and her kittens."

He put Cat and her kittens in a basket and tied the cover down. He rode over to the McDonald's ranch.

Mrs. McDonald was glad to have Cat and her kittens. Her cat was getting old. He did not catch mice any more.

Mrs. McDonald fixed a box on the porch. Then Jimmie put Cat and her four little black kittens into the box.

Jimmie was very sad as he rode back across the river. But he was glad that Cat and her family of kittens had a good home. He knew the cowboys would miss the black cat and the family of kittens.

This is not the end of the story.

Two days later, Mrs. Jones got up early to make breakfast for the cowboys. She was going to throw Cat's box away. But when she went to the corner of the kitchen to get the box, there was a very wet black cat in the box and four little black kittens. They were all sound asleep.

Cat opened her eyes and looked up at Mrs. Jones and meowed as if to say, "I brought my babies back home. Don't send me away again. Please let me stay."

Mrs. Jones dried Cat's fur and gave her some warm milk.

When the cowboys came to breakfast, Mrs. Jones said, "Cat and her kittens are back home. I guess she will have to stay."

The cowboys could hardly believe that so little a cat could have walked all those miles and swam across the river, carrying a kitten in her mouth. She could only carry one kitten at a time and the McDonald ranch was ten miles away.

"I think Cat is the bravest little animal I have ever known," said Jimmie.